To Jeffrey —

Who sleeps under

the same star.

Alec Dann

Half a Moon and One Whole Star

by Crescent Dragonwagon
illustrations by Jerry Pinkney

Macmillan Publishing Company
New York

Macmillan Publishing Company
866 Third Avenue, New York, N.Y. 10022
Collier Macmillan Canada, Inc.

Printed and bound by South China Printing Company, Hong Kong
First American Edition
10 9 8 7 6 5 4 3 2 1

The text of this book is set in 16 pt. Goudy Old Style.
The illustrations are rendered in watercolor pastel and colored
pencil on paper and reproduced in full color.

Library of Congress Cataloging in Publication Data
Dragonwagon, Crescent.
Half a moon and one whole star.
Summary: The summer night is full of wonderful
sounds and scents as Susan falls asleep.
[1. Night—Fiction. 2. Sleep—Fiction. 3. Stories
in rhyme] I. Pinkney, Jerry, ill. II. Title.
PZ8.3.D77Hal 1986 [E] 85-13818
ISBN 0-02-733120-2

For Susan Sims Smith, awakening.
—C.D.

For my granddaughter, Gloria Nicole.
—J.P.

Up above the earth so far
Hang half a moon and one whole star
Hang one whole star and half a moon:
Nighttime will be coming soon.

Robins fold their wings in sleep
Parrots rest in jungles deep

Chickens in their hen house, drowsing
Owls and bats are just now rousing
Possums sniffing, night frogs leaping

Susan lies in bed, not sleeping.
Not yet sleeping, but does she doze,
Blinking as the curtain blows?
Yes, yes, yes, she does, sleep, Susan, sleep.

Outside her window, summer night
And summer scents and summer's right
For honeysuckle, green-cut lawns
Susan breathes green smells and yawns
Susan hears the crickets whir
Susan sees the curtains stir
Sees them stir through half-closed eyes
Hears the Steinkamps call good-byes
Half-closed eyes are drooping low
She hears laughter down below
On the porch her parents talk

Whir
Whir
Whir

In the woods, the raccoons walk.
In the lake, the wet dark deep,
Do minnows flash though sound asleep?
Yes, yes, yes, they do, sleep, Susan, sleep.

CLUB
DANCE

Tonight, the docked ship in the bay
Will raise its anchor, sail away
And walking down a street alone
Comes Johnny with his saxophone
He'll play it black and blue and right
And at the club they'll dance tonight
He'll play while bakers bake their bread
While Susan turns and dreams in bed.

Will morning glories, closed up tight,
Conceal their blueness through the night?
Yes, yes, yes, they will, sleep, Susan, sleep.

The ship is on the ocean now
With one lone sailor on the prow
Who sees one star and half a moon
Who knows daybreak is coming soon
Who thinks of distant coral coves
As bakers count their golden loaves
As Johnny packs his saxophone
And, whistling softly, heads for home

As Susan's parents sleep, their room
Is lit up by one half a moon.
Does Susan dream of music, bread,
Of oceans, as she sleeps in bed?
Yes, yes, yes, she does,
sleep, Susan, sleep.

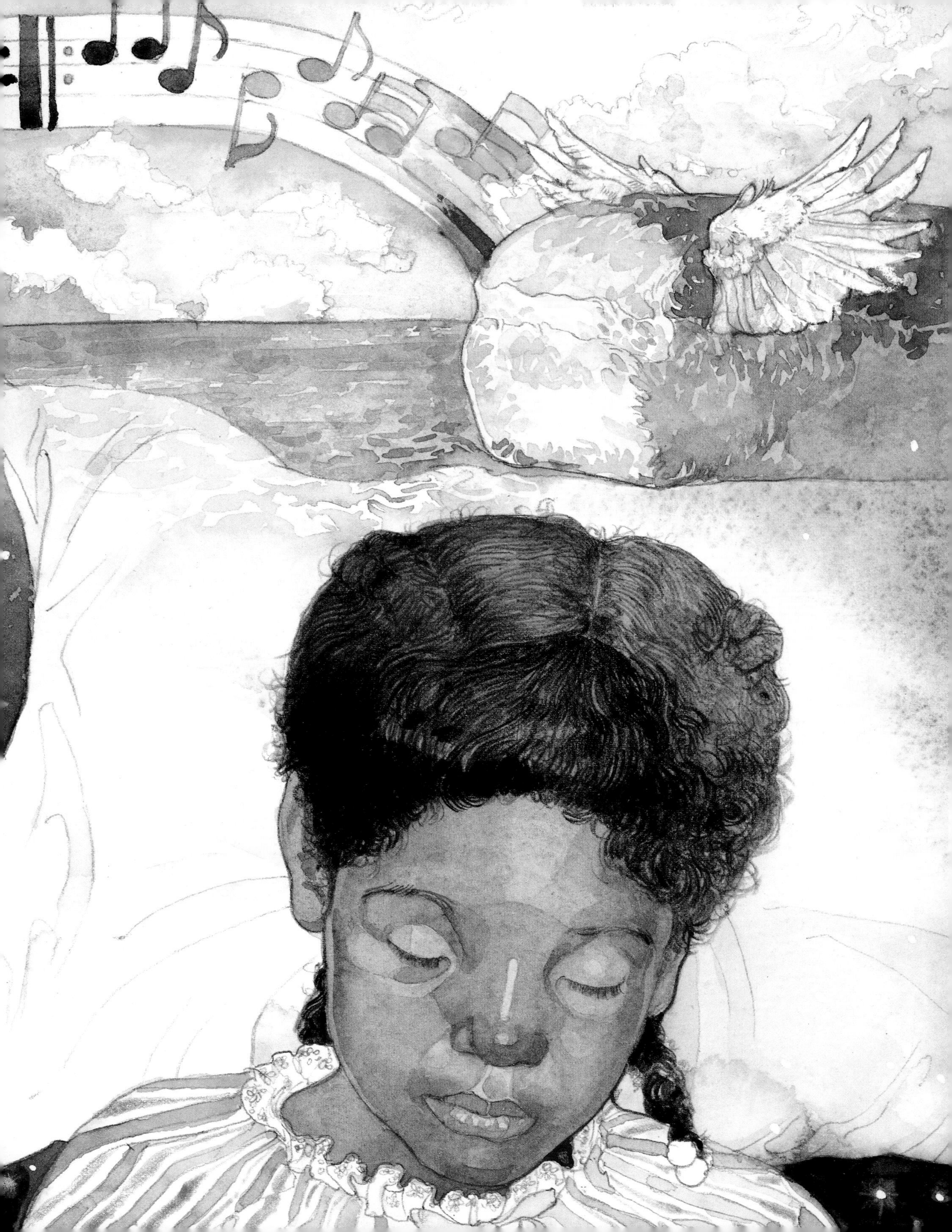

And when the night begins to pale
The possum, drowsy, curls his tail
The owl will land, the chickens stir
The crickets cease their night-long whir
And with the notes inside his head
Johnny will climb into bed

As will the bakers, white with flour
As will the sailor in just an hour
For though the day has not begun
The sky will hint of coming sun.
And when the sky hints, won't the sun rise?
Yes, but not yet, close your eyes.
Yes, yes, yes, day soon, sleep, Susan, sleep.

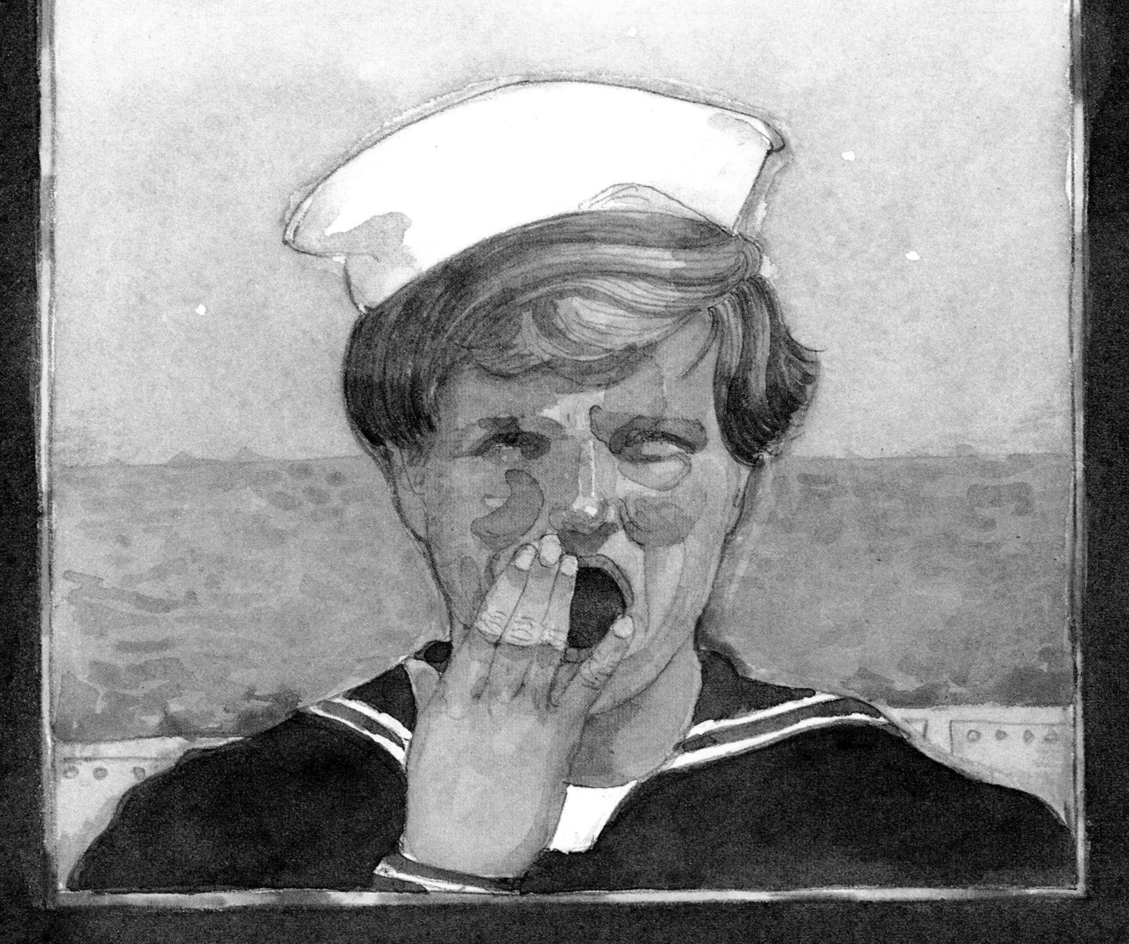

And in the morning when she wakes
Susan will eat breakfast cakes
And breakfast breads at breakfast hour
The morning glories full in flower
Her parents drinking orange juice
Her summer nightgown light and loose

No star to see but half a moon
That falls and fades and will go soon
A rising shining summer sun
Another summer day begun.
And won't she swim and run and play
And eat ice cream this summer's day?
Yes, yes, yes, she will, but now,
sleep, Susan, sleep.

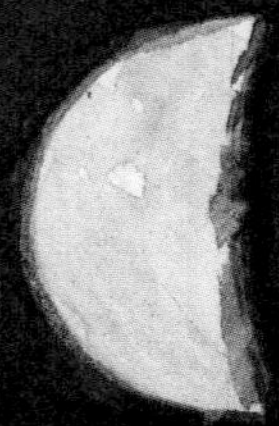

Up above the earth so far
Hang half a moon and one whole star
Hang one whole star and half a moon:
Nighttime will be coming soon.
But where there's night there's day to follow
Sleep Susan sleep, for come tomorrow
Above the earth there will be one
Hotly glowing summer sun
Round and orange, like a ball
Like moon and star, you'll have them all!
So sleep, Susan, sleep.